Monsters are afraid
of the MOON

Published by Bloomsbury Publishing, New York, London, and Berlin
Distributed to the trade by Holtzbrinck Publishers

Library of Congress Cataloging-in-Publication Data
Satrapi, Marjane.
[Monstres n'aiment pas la lune]
Monsters are afraid of the moon / by Marjane Satrapi ; [translated by Jill Davis].—1st U.S. ed.
p.   cm.
Summary: When Marie brings the moon into her bedroom, it scares away the monsters who have
tormented her but also causes problems which only the village cats can help solve.
ISBN-10: 1-58234-744-1 • ISBN-13: 978-1-58234-744-8
[1. Fairy tales. 2. Moon—Fiction. 3. Monsters—Fiction. 4. Cats—Fiction.] I. Davis, Jill. II. Title.
PZ8.S264Mon 2006   [E]—dc22   2006002152

First U.S. Edition 2006
Printed in China
1 3 5 7 9 10 8 6 4 2

Bloomsbury Publishing, Children's Books, U.S.A.
175 Fifth Avenue, New York, NY 10010

All papers used by Bloomsbury Publishing are natural, recyclable products
made from wood grown in well-managed forests. The manufacturing processes
conform to the environmental regulations of the country of origin.

MoNSterS are afraid
of the MOON

Marjane Satrapi

BLOOMSBURY
CHILDREN'S
BOOKS

Once upon a time, there lived a little girl named Marie. Marie loved having fun all day long.

She picked cherries from her cherry tree, played with her kitty cat, read funny stories, and drew pictures of bunnies.

But when the sun set each night, everything changed.

You see, as soon as Marie climbed into bed, three of the scariest monsters who ever lived would come out from the shadows.

The first scary monster would pinch her right on the nose. The second scary monster would pull her hair. And the third scary monster would stick out his tongue and go cross-eyed.

Marie didn't know what to do. If she hid, the monsters always found her. And she just didn't have the strength to fight all three. She had to come up with an idea.

One night, Marie looked up and noticed that the sky was lit up by the moon. "Aha!" she said to herself. "Since monsters come out only at night, they must be afraid of the light. I'll bring the moon into my room tonight, and they'll never bother me again!"

She took a huge pair of scissors, cut the moon out of the sky, and put it inside a lovely bird cage over her bed.

Her plan worked perfectly.
The monsters left Marie alone.

But out in the streets, the moon had disappeared. Suddenly, all the cats in the village were in total darkness and they couldn't see a thing.

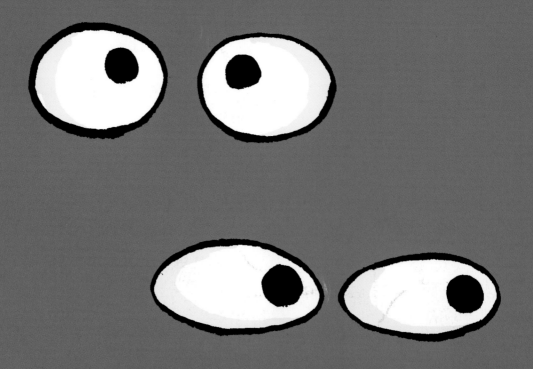

In the dark, they bumped into everything! At first there were dozens—then hundreds—of cats in the hospital for a bump on the head, a scratch on the ear, or a broken paw.

But the moon's disappearance
made some creatures happy.
The rats, who were used to dark
sewers, were no longer frightened
of the cats in the neighborhood.

The rats became the kings of the streets—stealing treats from the market, gnawing at doors and walls, and yowling until the early morning. Soon, not only had the rats ruined the entire village, they had woken everyone up!

The situation became intolerable. The cats decided to see their king, explain the predicament, and ask for his help.

So his majesty the Cat King, accompanied by his cabinet minister, went to see Marie.

"Marie," said his majesty, "we cats can no longer go out at night. The rats have taken over the streets, and now they are not afraid of anyone. You must return the moon to the sky!"

"But if I return the moon to the sky," Marie said, "are those horrible monsters going to come back? The moon is the only thing that keeps them away because it makes my room light at night. Without the moon, I'll be afraid again."

The Cat King said, "The moon is not the only answer. Did you know that monsters are also afraid of cats? I will send one of my soldiers to stay with you at night. He will sleep at the foot of your bed and that will keep the horrible creatures away. In exchange, you must give back the moon."

Marie thought for a moment,

and then she agreed.

So when you see a little girl with a cat sleeping at the foot of her bed, now you will know why.

THE  END

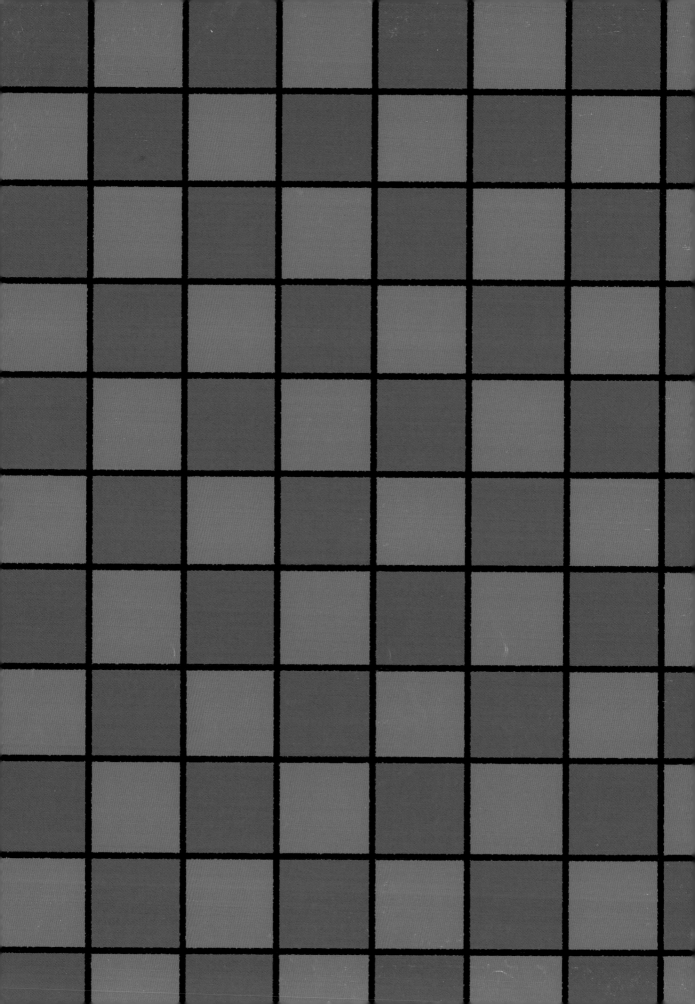